AN EGG FOR SHABBAT

Mirik Snir

Illustrated by **Eleyor Snir**

KAR-BEN
PUBLISHING

KAR-BEN PUBLISHING®
An imprint of Lerner Publishing Group, Inc.
241 First Avenue North
Minneapolis, MN 55401 USA
Website address: www.karben.com

Main body text set in Billy Infant semibold.
Typeface provided by SparkyType.

Library of Congress Cataloging-in-Publication Data

Names: Snir, Mirik, author. | Snir, Eleyor, 1975–illustrator.
Title: An egg for Shabbat / by Mirik Snir ; illustrated by Elyor Snir.
Description: Minneapolis : Kar-Ben Publishing, [2021] | Audience:
    Ages 4–7. | Audience: Grades K–1. | Summary: Young Ben,
    eager to help his mother, rushes to the chicken pen Sunday
    through Friday mornings and each day learns a new lesson
    about carrying an egg.
Identifiers: LCCN 2020014833 (print) | LCCN 2020014834 (ebook) |
    ISBN 9781541596641 (library binding) | ISBN 9781541596658
    (paperback) | ISBN 9781728417622 (ebook)
Subjects: CYAC: Stories in rhyme. | Eggs—Fiction. | Helpfulness—
    Fiction. | Jews—Fiction. | Mothers and sons—Fiction.
Classification: LCC PZ8.3.S4686 Egg 2021 (print) | LCC
    PZ8.3.S4686 (ebook) | DDC [E]—dc23

LC record available at https://lccn.loc.gov/2020014833
LC ebook record available at https://lccn.loc.gov/2020014834

PJ Library Edition ISBN 978-1-72843-889-4

Manufactured in China
1-49680-49596-10/2/2020

042125.5K1/B1628/A3

For Sol, Eliana, Gala, and Emilia
Love, Imma Eleyor and Savta Mirik

SUNDAY

On Sunday morning, Mom said,

"Ben!
Please fetch me
an egg
from the
chicken pen."

With a happy yelp,
Ben went off to help.

He couldn't resist.
He wanted to play.

"This looks like a ball,"
he thought right away.

And then . . . **oh no!**

With a big *smash*, the egg came down —*crash!*

The boy came home.
His eyes were sad.

He told his mom.
Would she be mad?

"Oh, Ben, my dear. Oh, son of mine. You learned a lesson, and that's fine."

MONDAY

On Monday morning, Mom said,

"Ben!
Please fetch me
an egg
from the
chicken pen."

With a happy yelp,
Ben went off to help.

"I'll give it a try . . ."
the little boy said.

"I can carry some things
on the top of my head."

And then . . . **oh no!**

**Hop, pop, kerplop!
The egg did drop.**

The boy came home.
His eyes were sad.

He told his mom.
Would she be mad?

"Oh, Ben,
my dear.
Oh, son of mine.
You learned a lesson,
and that's fine."

TUESDAY

On Tuesday morning, Mom said,

"Ben!
Please fetch me
an egg
from the
chicken pen."

With a happy yelp,
Ben went off to help.

"I will hold the egg tight,
bring it home in one piece.

Not a dent, not a crack,
not a scratch or a crease."

And then . . . **oh no!**

**Clickety-clack!
The egg
did crack.**

The boy came home.
His eyes were sad.

He told his mom.
Would she be mad?

"Oh, Ben,
my dear.
Oh, son of mine.
You learned a lesson,
and that's fine."

WEDNESDAY

On Wednesday morning, Mom said,

"Ben!
Please fetch me
an egg
from the
chicken pen."

With a happy yelp,
Ben went off to help.

Too fast went Ben—
until he tripped.

"I'll take this home!"
He ran and skipped.

And then . . . **oh no!**

Clash and **clatter!**
The egg went *splatter.*

The boy came home.
His eyes were sad.

He told his mom.
Would she be mad?

"Oh, Ben,
my dear.
Oh, son of mine.
You learned a lesson,
and that's fine."

THURSDAY

On Thursday morning, Mom said,

"Ben!
Please fetch me
an egg
from the
chicken pen."

With a happy yelp,
Ben went off to help.

Ben thought to himself,
"I'll just peek inside . . .

and look for the chick.
Where does it hide?"

And then . . . **oh no!**

Flickety-flake!
The egg did break.

The boy came home.
His eyes were sad.

He told his mom.
Would she be mad?

"Oh, Ben,
my dear.
Oh, son of mine.
You learned a lesson,
and that's fine."

FRIDAY

On Friday morning, Mom said,

"Ben! Please fetch me an egg from the chicken pen."

With a happy yelp,
Ben went off to help.

"I have the egg!"
Ben shouted loudly.

What did Mom do?

She hugged him proudly!
"I braided two challahs,
dear son of mine.
The egg you brought
will make them shine."

On Friday night, their eyes were bright.

The challahs gleamed
with special light.

SATURDAY

**And on Shabbat,
the day of rest,
they gathered strength
. . . for what?**

You guessed!

SUNDAY

Might Mom need
his help again?

Sunday

Monday

Tuesday

Wednesday

Thursday

Friday

**Saturday
(Shabbat)**